"You never come in th[...] said Posey.

"This is a special night." Gramps helped Mrs. Romero off with her coat. "I thought we should do it right."

Posey's mom came out of the kitchen with Danny.

"Dad, Norma," she said. "You better tell us your news fast or Posey's going to burst."

Gramps coughed. He took Mrs. Romero's hand.

"I asked Norma to be my wife, and she said yes," he said.

"I knew it! I knew it!" Posey shouted. "You're getting married!" Posey jumped up and down. She twirled around. "I told you so, Mom!" she cried.

Read all the books starring
PRINCESS P*SEY, FIRST GRADER!

PRINCESS POSEY

and the

FLOWER GIRL FIASCO

Stephanie Greene

ILLUSTRATED BY

Stephanie Roth Sisson

PUFFIN BOOKS

To Posey readers everywhere. —S.G.

For Stephanie Greene, Susan Kochan,
Marikka Tamura, and Cecilia Yung.
Thank you. —S.R.S.

PUFFIN BOOKS
An imprint of Penguin Random House LLC
375 Hudson Street
New York, New York 10014

Published simultaneously in the United States of America
by G. P. Putnam's Sons and Puffin Books, imprints of Penguin Random House LLC, 2018

LIBRARY OF CONGRESS CATALOGING-IN-PUBLICATION DATA IS AVAILABLE.

Puffin Books ISBN 9780147517203

Printed in the United States of America

1 3 5 7 9 10 8 6 4 2

CONTENTS

CHAPTER ONE

HENRY'S BIG NEWS

It was show-and-tell time.

"Who has something they would like to share with the class?" said Miss Lee.

Henry's hand shot up.

"Go ahead, Henry," she told him.

"We're moving to a new house," Henry said.

"That's very exciting," said Miss Lee.

"I like our house now." Henry frowned.

"I'm sure you're going to like your new house, too," said Miss Lee. "Where is it?"

"I don't know. I didn't see it yet."

"Will you still go to our school?" said Ava.

"Will you still be in our class?" Posey asked.

"My mom said yes," said Henry.

"That's wonderful." Miss Lee smiled around the circle. "We will look forward to hearing about Henry's new house, won't we, class?"

Everyone nodded.

Except Posey.

She felt sorry for Henry.

Posey never wanted to move from her house.

She loved her bedroom and her backyard.

She liked the way the kitchen door slammed when she ran outside. She liked the feeling of the wooden deck under her bare feet in the summer.

She liked having Nick and Tyler on one side, too. And Mrs. Romero and her dog, Hero, on the other side.

Posey never wanted any of that to change.

EVEN BIGGER NEWS

Posey's mom picked her up after school.

"How come you aren't at work?" Posey asked when she got in the car.

"I want to make a special dinner," her mom said. "Gramps and Mrs. Romero are coming. Gramps said they have something to tell us."

"What do you think it is?" said Posey.

"I don't know. We'll have to wait and see."

"I bet they're getting married," Posey said.

Her mom laughed. "You've been saying that for months."

"I bet they are."

They got what they needed at the grocery store. Posey picked out a mix to make a cake.

Danny tried to grab candy in the checkout line the way he always did.

When they got home, Posey set the table. She folded the napkins so they looked fancy.

She wrote everyone's name on a piece of paper and put it where they would sit.

Then she went upstairs and put on her pink tutu and her favorite star necklace. When the front doorbell rang, she ran to open the door.

It was Gramps and Mrs. Romero.

"You never come in the front door, Gramps!" said Posey.

"This is a special night." Gramps helped Mrs. Romero off with her coat. "I thought we should do it right."

Posey's mom came out of the kitchen with Danny.

"Dad, Norma," she said. "You better tell us your news fast or Posey's going to burst."

Gramps coughed. He took Mrs. Romero's hand.

"I asked Norma to be my wife, and she said yes," he said.

"I knew it! I knew it!" Posey shouted. "You're getting married!"

Posey jumped up and down. She twirled around. "I told you so, Mom!" she cried.

Her mom kissed Gramps and Mrs. Romero. They both kissed Posey and Danny.

Everyone was laughing and talking when they sat down to dinner.

"When is the wedding?" Posey's mom asked.

"We don't want to waste any time, do we, Norma?" said Gramps.

"We were hoping for a simple ceremony in your backyard next Saturday," Mrs. Romero said.

"We'd be honored," said Posey's mom.

"Can I be the flower girl and pick whatever flowers I want?" Posey said.

"Absolutely," said Gramps.

"You and I can go shopping for them," said Mrs. Romero.

Posey suddenly felt shy. "Does this mean you'll be my grandmother?" she asked.

"Only if you want me to," said Mrs. Romero.

After Gramps and Mrs. Romero left, Posey went upstairs to get ready for bed. Her mom came to tuck her in.

"No book tonight?" she asked.

"I used up all my energy being excited," said Posey. She yawned.

"I'm not surprised," said her mom.

"What will I call Mrs. Romero?" Posey said.

"You two will have to work that out."

Posey curled up on her side. "It's like a fairy tale, except with gray-haired people," she said.

"It certainly is," said her mom. "I'm very happy for Gramps."

"I'm happy for us, too," said Posey.

CHAPTER
THREE

THE PERFECT
WEDDING PRESENT

Posey told her friends when she got to school the next day.

"I was a flower girl when my aunt got married," said Ava. "She was so beautiful."

"Mrs. Romero's beautiful, too," said Posey.

"I didn't know grandparents got married," said Grace. "They're so old."

"Gramps is sixty," Posey said.

"Sixty! That's much older than fifty!" said Nikki.

"Is Danny going to carry the rings?" said Ava. "My little cousin did that. They were on a pillow."

"My mom's afraid that Danny will bury them in his sandbox," said Posey.

"He might even eat them," said Grace.

The girls giggled.

"Your gramps and Mrs. Romero couldn't get married if he did that," Nikki said.

Posey didn't want that to happen. She was so excited that Mrs. Romero was going to be her grandmother.

During math, Posey tried to pay attention. But she wanted it to be art time so she could draw a picture.

When it was, she hurried to get markers and paper. She drew Gramps and Mrs. Romero and Hero in the house next door. Then she drew herself and Danny and her mom in their own yard. She drew a huge heart around all of them.

She wrote "My Family" at the top of the paper.

Miss Lee asked what the picture was about. Posey told her.

"You're a lucky girl," Miss Lee said.

"I'm giving the picture to Gramps and Mrs. Romero," said Posey.

"It will be a perfect wedding present," said Miss Lee.

"That's what it is, a wedding present," said Posey.

"I'm sure they will love it."

Posey was sure they would, too.

CHAPTER
FOUR

"HERO, TOO?"

Posey showed the picture to her mom when she came home from work.

"Can we buy a frame for it?" Posey asked.

"Me see," said Danny. He tried to grab the paper.

"Danny, don't!" Posey said. "You will tear it."

"Here, Danny, play with this." Posey's mom pulled a pot with a lid out of the cabinet. She gave them to him. "Be a parade," she said.

Danny loved to watch parades on television. He'd bang a pot and lid together and march with them.

"Take the parade into the living room," Mom told him.

Danny marched out of the kitchen, banging all the way.

"Okay." Posey's mom sat at the table and smoothed Posey's picture in front of her.

"That's you and me and Danny," Posey said. She pointed. "And that's Gramps and Mrs. Romero and Hero. They live in Mrs. Romero's house."

"It's a wonderful picture, Posey," her mom said. "But I have something to tell you."

"What?"

"Mrs. Romero and Gramps are going to live at Gramps's house."

"At Gramps's house?" Posey's

eyes got as big as quarters. "You mean Hero, too?"

"Hero, too," said her mom.

"No fair! Why can't Gramps live in Mrs. Romero's house?" Posey cried.

"His place is much bigger," said her mom. "Think of how happy Hero will be with that big yard to run around in."

"He won't be happy! He won't have me!" Posey started to cry. "Tell Mrs. Romero not to sell her house."

"I'm afraid she already has."

Posey put her head on her arms.
"I wish Gramps had never met
Mrs. Romero!" she wailed.

"You love Mrs. Romero," her mom said.

"I don't anymore! I don't! Gramps won't visit us all the time. I won't get to see Hero."

Nothing her mom said made Posey feel better.

Posey went upstairs after dinner and got into bed. She didn't want to take a bath or read a book.

Her mom came to say good night. She said Posey would feel better tomorrow.

But Posey was never going to feel better.

Hero wouldn't know where she was if he moved. He would think Posey didn't love him anymore.

She squeezed her eyes shut.

Posey didn't want Mrs. Romero to be her grandmother.

She wasn't going to call her anything.

CHAPTER
FIVE

"IT WON'T BE
THE SAME"

Gramps came to take Posey to school the next morning.

"Remember, no long faces," her mom said. She handed Posey her lunch bag. "Gramps deserves to be happy. You can see Hero whenever you want."

"It won't be the same," said Posey.

She went outside and got into Gramps's truck.

"Morning," he said. He backed down the driveway. "Your mom said she's going to buy you a new dress for the wedding."

"I know," Posey said.

"Mrs. Romero wants to buy you a pair of shoes to go with it," said Gramps.

"I don't want new shoes."

Gramps raised his eyebrows. "Even if they match your dress?"

Posey shook her head.

"How about you two picking out your flowers this afternoon?"

"I don't care what kind they are," said Posey.

"You don't?" Gramps looked at her for a long minute. "If that's how you feel, I will pass that information along."

❁ ❁ ❁

Posey went straight to her table when she got to Miss Lee's room. She didn't want to tell her friends about Hero yet. She knew it would make her cry.

Henry was already there.

"Did you see your new house yet?" Posey asked.

"No. My dad said it has a dog-house in the backyard, so we're getting a dog," Henry said.

"Doesn't he know you're afraid of dogs?" said Posey.

"He said I won't be afraid when I get used to it. My sister said she wouldn't move unless she could have one. We're getting a small one."

"A small dog will be good," said Posey. "You can hold it in your lap."

"That will make it easier for it to bite me," said Henry.

✿ ✿ ✿

At recess, Posey cried when she told
Ava and Nikki and Grace about
Mrs. Romero and Hero moving.

Nikki held her hand. Grace
patted her face.

"Mrs. Romero is mean," Ava said.

"She's selfish," said Grace. "That's what my mom calls my brother when he takes all the cookies."

"Maybe your mom will buy you a dog," Nikki said.

They made her feel a little better. But Posey didn't want a different dog.

She only wanted Hero.

CHAPTER
SIX

"I DON'T WANT TO"

"I got some boxes for Mrs. Romero to use for packing," Posey's mom said when they got home from school. "After you have a snack, you can help me carry them over to her."

"I don't want to," said Posey.

"You don't? Mrs. Romero might appreciate some help."

"I don't want to."

"You love helping her," said her mom.

Posey shook her head.

"Okay. I won't be long."

Posey didn't go to Mrs. Romero's house the next day, either.

She didn't see her for the rest of the week.

On Saturday morning, Posey went outside to ride her bike.

Mrs. Romero was sitting on their back steps.

"Long time no see," she said. She patted the step beside her. "Sit down for a minute."

Posey sat.

"This has all happened very quickly, hasn't it?" Mrs. Romero smiled. "Gramps and me and the wedding."

Posey nodded.

"I know you're going to miss Hero," said Mrs. Romero. "I bet you think it's no fair I'm getting both him and Gramps."

"How did you see inside my head?" Posey asked.

"I didn't. I know what's inside your heart." Mrs. Romero hugged Posey tight. "How would you like to have Hero live here for a while?"

Posey sat up straight. "With me?
In my own house?"

"I talked to your mom. She's
willing to try it."

"It will make Hero so happy!"
Posey shouted. She jumped to her
feet. "I will walk him and feed him
and everything! Mom won't have
to do anything!"

Posey's mom came onto the porch. "I see you told her," she said to Mrs. Romero.

"Hero's going to live with us!" Posey shouted.

"It may not work out, Posey," said her mom.

"It will, it will, I promise!"

"Norma, I hope you're sure," said Posey's mom.

"I am." Mrs. Romero stood up. "I couldn't bear it if this marriage made anyone unhappy."

CHAPTER SEVEN

HERO COMES
TO STAY

The wedding was so much fun.

Nick and Tyler came. So did some of the neighbors.

Posey carried a bouquet of blue and pink flowers.

The minister said, "You may now kiss the bride."

Nick and Tyler both said, "Gross." Everyone laughed.

They ate hamburgers and hot dogs. One of the neighbors had made a wedding cake with six layers.

Everyone stayed until it was dark. Then it was time for Gramps and Mrs. Romero to leave.

"See you next week," Mrs. Romero called as they pulled out.

Posey and her mom and Danny waved until they were gone.

"Come on, Hero," Posey said. "You're sleeping in my room."

Posey had put Hero's bed on the floor next to hers. She brushed her teeth and got into bed.

"Good
night, Hero.
Sleep tight,"
she said.

Hero got
up and went to the door. He
scratched to go out.

"No, Hero,
you sleep
here now."

Posey got up and led him back to his bed by his collar.

"Lie down," she said.

As soon as Posey got back in

bed, Hero got up again and went to the door.

No matter how many times she

told him, Hero wouldn't stay in his bed.

"What are you doing still awake?" her mom asked when she opened the door.

"Hero won't go to sleep," said Posey.

"I think we have to let him sleep downstairs. That's where he slept at Mrs. Romero's house."

"But I want him to sleep with me."

"Let's give him a few days to get used to living here," said her mom. She led Hero downstairs.

The next morning, Posey found Hero sleeping by the kitchen door. She took his leash off the hook and snapped it onto his collar.

"Come on. Let's go play," she said.

Hero followed her down the steps. Posey headed toward Nick and Tyler's house.

Hero pulled in the other direction.

"No, Hero, you don't live there anymore, remember?" said Posey.

Her mom came out to the driveway with Danny.

"Hero thinks he still lives in Mrs. Romero's house," Posey told her.

"Give him time," said her mom. "He'll get used to it."

CHAPTER EIGHT

HOMESICK

Hero tried to go to Mrs. Romero's house the next day, too.

And the next.

When Posey threw his ball, Hero didn't run after it.

When they went inside, he lay down next to the kitchen door.

He didn't eat any of his food.

"What do you think is wrong with Hero?" Posey asked after dinner one night. She was coloring while her mom cleaned the kitchen.

"I don't know. What do you think?" said her mom.

"Maybe he has a temperature," Posey said.

"Maybe."

Posey colored in another flower. "Or maybe he ate something bad."

"He doesn't seem to be eating much of anything, does he?" Her mom finished drying a pot. She put it in the cabinet.

"I miss the old Hero, don't you, Mom?"

"I do."

Posey colored more. "Do you think Mrs. Romero misses him?"

"I'm pretty sure she does."

"She had him for a long time, didn't she?"

"Since he was a puppy."

Posey put her blue crayon back in the box and picked a yellow one. She colored the same petal on a flower for a long time. She frowned, like it was hard work.

"What do you think we should do?" Posey said at last.

"I don't know. What do you think?"

Posey knew her mom was looking at her. She didn't want to look up.

She didn't want to say the words out loud.

She remembered how she felt
when she heard Hero was moving.
That he wouldn't know where she
was.

That he would think Posey
didn't love him anymore.

Instead, he thought Mrs. Romero didn't love him.

Posey's eyes were stinging when she looked up. "I think we have to give him back to Mrs. Romero," she said.

CHAPTER NINE

HOME AGAIN

Posey's mom turned into Gramps's driveway.

Posey had put on her pink tutu before they left. It would help her be strong like Princess Posey. Strong enough to give Hero back.

He was lying on the seat between her and Danny. Posey kept her hand on Hero's back the whole ride.

When her mom stopped the car, Posey opened her door to let Hero out.

"Hero!" cried Mrs. Romero.

Hero went crazy. He ran to Mrs. Romero and almost knocked her over. She knelt down and put her arms around Hero's neck.

He licked her face all over.

When she let him go, Hero ran
to Posey. Then to Gramps. Then to
Posey's mom and Danny and back
to Mrs. Romero again.

They all laughed.

"He's checking to make
sure his whole family
is here," said
Gramps.

It was impossible to be sad when Hero was so happy.

When he finally calmed down, they went inside.

"Come with me," Mrs. Romero said to Posey. "I have something to show you."

They went upstairs. A sign on one of the bedroom doors said "Posey's Room."

The room had a bed and a bookshelf. Three small windows looked over the field behind the house.

"Is it really my own room?" said
Posey.

"You can paint it any color you want," Mrs. Romero said.

Posey ran downstairs.

"Mrs. Romero wants me to spend the night so we can buy paint for my room," she told her mom. "Can I?"

"Sure." Her mom picked up Danny.

"We'll bring her home in the morning," said Gramps.

❁ ❁ ❁

It took Posey a long time to pick out the color she wanted at the hardware store. She finally chose purple. Mrs. Romero said she would make purple striped curtains to match.

They went to the counter to pay.

"That's quite a color you picked out," the cashier said.

"Posey's grandfather told her she can have any color she wants," Mrs. Romero said.

"My gran is making curtains to match," Posey said. She looked at Mrs. Romero. "Is it okay to call you that?" she whispered.

"It's better than okay. I love it."

Mrs. Romero put her arm around Posey's shoulders. "I will get out my sewing machine the minute we get home," she said.

CHAPTER TEN

HENRY'S HOUSE

"**B**ye, Gramps! Bye, Gran!" Posey called. Gramps tooted the horn as they pulled out of her driveway.

Posey headed for the kitchen door. Suddenly, she heard a high *yap!*

Yap!

Posey looked at Mrs. Romero's yard.

A little black puppy was standing beside the hedge. It was the smallest dog Posey had ever seen. It looked like a tiny bundle of fur.

Posey ran over and picked it up. She held it carefully against her chest. It didn't even weigh as much as a feather.

The puppy licked Posey's face with its tiny pink tongue.

"That tickles," Posey said.

"Winnie, come back!" a voice called.

A tall boy with dark hair ran into Posey's yard.

"Henry!" Posey shouted. "What are you doing here?"

"This is my new house," he said.

"That means you live next door to me!" said Posey.

Henry took Winnie from her. "Good thing you found her," he said. "Stella would kill me if I lost her."

Winnie licked Henry's face, too. He laughed.

"You're not afraid of dogs anymore," said Posey.

"You want to come see where Winnie sleeps?" said Henry.

"Hold on! I have to ask my

mom." Posey raced up the steps and into their kitchen.

"Mom!" she shouted. "Can I go to Henry's house?"

Her mom came in from the living room. "Who's Henry?" she asked.

"He's my friend. He wants to show me where Winnie sleeps," Posey told her.

"Who's Winnie?" Her mom sounded confused.

"Henry's dog," said Posey.

"Where does Henry live?"

"Next door! Where do you

think?" Sometimes her mom didn't understand anything.

"Oh, I see." Her mom laughed. "So now it's Henry's house."

"Can I go?" Posey repeated.

"Sure."

Posey ran back outside. "Henry," she shouted. "Wait for me!"